Cut Me Some Slack, Lord
Reflections For Teen Males

by Mary Ann Kerl

LANGMARC PUBLISHING
AUSTIN, TEXAS

Cut Me Some Slack, Lord:
Reflections For Teen Males
By Mary Ann Kerl

Copyright © Mary Ann Kerl 2004
First Printing: 2004
Cover Photo and Interior Photographs: Susan Reue
Cover Graphics: Michael Qualben
First Edition

Thank you to Andrew, Ryan, and Rachel
for use of their photographs.

Printed in the United States of America.

Unless otherwise specified, Scripture quotations are from
the Holy Bible, New International Verson.
Copyright © 1973, 1978, 1984 International Bible Society.
Used by permission of Zondervan Bible Publishers.

Specified paraphrased verses are from
The Living Bible.
Copyright © 1971 by Tyndale House Publishers,
Wheaton, Illinois 60187.

LangMarc Publishing
P.O. 90488
Austin, Texas 78709-0488
Orders: 1-800-864-1648

Library of Congress Control Number 2004104344
ISBN: 1-880-292-521 $9.95

Contents

Miracle Gifts
- One "Humongous" Miracle 9
- Check Out That Dude in the Mirror 11
- A Hero Accepts Himself 13

Ego Issues
- Is It Cowardly to Cry? 17
- When Life Gives You a Bum Rap 19
- Happiness—Check it Out! 21

Popularity Issues
- Friendship Is God's Idea 23
- Promises to Friends 25
- Is It Okay for Guys to Have Fun? 27
- What About Drugs? 29
- Forgive Others—and Yourself 31

Think Positive
- Brag, Brag, Brag! 33
- Life Can Be Such a Puzzle 35
- Dealing With Change 37
- Let Me Think 39

One Day at a Time
- A Place and a Time to Daydream 43
- Deal With the Present—Today 45
- Research a Future Career 47
- Give Yourself a Break 49

Appearance and Dating
- What Makes a Guy Good-looking Anyway? 51
- What's the Big Deal with Self-Esteem? 53
- Attracting Girls 55
- Love and Money—Do They Mix? 57
- What About Sex? 59
- What About Abortion? 61
- What About Homosexuality? 63

Parent Problems
- Running Away From Home 65
- Making Demands on Parents 67
- When Your Parents Divorce 69
- What About a Stepparent? 71
- When a Parent Dies 73

Tools for Living
- Patience—What's That? 77
- Stress is so Stressful! 79
- When A Friend Dies 81

Current Issues
- Feeling Left Out 83
- Joining Cults 85
- The Horror of Terrorism 87
- What About Suicide? 89

Keep the Faith!
- Worship Only God 93
- What's the Big Deal About Faith? 95
- What's the Big Deal About Prayer? 97

Preface

Surely, every teen male at one time or another has stopped and wondered if he can't get a little slack. After all, it's not easy to grow up, especially in today's world with hot social issues like drugs, sex, gangs, and other types of peer pressure youth face today.

Good news!

Our Lord is willing to walk by your side in your teen years to cut you some slack and give guidance. Explore the experiences of the young men in their true stories of their personal predicaments. Allow their Christian examples to give you guidance in your own personal life. That's the way God works through other people.

We'd feel pretty alone if we were the only person who ever faced a certain crisis. We're not. You can be certain that whatever circumstance you're in as you read this, some other young person has been there before you. The people featured in this book found the answer: the Lord *is* with you—always! He will help you face the stormy seas if you call on Him. Sometimes you may not feel His presence but, as Christians, the Bible gives confirmation to the fact that God is always with us no matter what and, indeed, he will help you through the difficult times in your life. He will cut you some slack.

So whatever problems you're having—maybe you're right smack in middle of a personal emergency as you read this—meditate on our reflections, which are designed to give Christian guidance in your life. Go ahead and take our challenges. They were devised to help you with daily Christian living.

Cut Me Some Slack, Lord is ideal for youth groups, Sunday School classes, and/or personal devotional materials. This book can be used with the girls' book of reflections, *Are You Listening, Lord?*

Cut Me Some Slack, Lord can be utilized as a tool for group discussion. Participants will enjoy stimulating conversations and therapeutic motivation for daily Christian living because of the carefully chosen topics especially for today's youth.

It is my prayer that, as you read this book, the Holy Spirit will reveal Jesus Christ to you in a special way that is personal and just right for today. Then you will know the Lord is with you and will cut you some slack.

Dedication

In memory of my father, Carl A. Heimbuch,
for his Christian love and support,
and to Michael Sauer,
a young Christian man
whose life touched many hearts.

One "Humongous" Miracle

What's the greatest gift you've ever received?

Now think about your answer. Was it yourself?

Concentrate on yourself for a moment. You are a gift—a great present from God to your parents and to the world. In fact, you're one "humongous" miracle!

God made you special. No one else is exactly like you. Even if people can be cloned some day, you're still unique with one distinct personality. No one else feels exactly like you do, shares all your hobbies and interests, or has your identical mannerisms. Even twins or other multiples have different intellects, tastes, and interests.

Isn't that terrific? Life would be boring if everyone was exactly alike. That would mean every person possesses the same talents, wants the same career, and likes the same girls. Imagine what disaster that would cause!

Considering you are a miracle, God wants you to love yourself. He desires for you to consider yourself in a special way. He wants you to treat your body and mind with respect. He wants you to avoid drugs, treat sexual desires with respect, and to live life to the fullest. Be productive. Do something great with your life.

In the Bible parable of the prodigal son (Luke 15:11-32), Jesus told how tragic a young man's life is that doesn't produce anything.

To make the right decisions for leading a productive Christian life, check out the scripture below.

❖SCRIPTURE:

"Trust in the Lord with all your heart and lean not on your own understanding; in all your ways acknowledge him, and he will make your paths straight." Proverbs 3:5,6

REFLECTION:

1) Think of the ways in which you're making some right decisions in your life.

2) Now think of the personal decisions you're making that may not be so wise. What can you do to change those unwise choices into wise ones that will put you on the Christian path?

CHALLENGE:

* Go for a jog today and contemplate on what a great person God made you.
* Before you go to bed tonight, thank God for making you, creating you into one neat human being.

CHECK OUT THAT DUDE IN THE MIRROR

Take a look at yourself in the mirror. Take note of how God made you. See how special He created you.

"Hey, are you kidding?" you may be saying to yourself. "What about my zits! Did God make those? Some gift! Thanks a lot, God!"

I doubt if zits were God's idea. It doesn't sound like God to give us something so painful emotionally in our growing-up years.

Actually when you think about it, zits and other physical characteristics aren't that important. What *is* important is how you look on the inside.

Look inside yourself. Find out who you are. A mirror shows us only how we look on the outside—if your hair is red, black, brown, or blonde. If your eyes are blue, green, hazel, or brown. Obviously a mirror can't show what's inside you. Only you can find out *who* you are.

Do you fly off the handle easily? Or do you have a mild nature, more inclined to go with the flow? What do you like to do? What *don't* you like to do? What are your favorite subjects in school? Your poorest?

After you've taken inventory of yourself, no doubt you will discover things you don't like about yourself as well as some things you do like. Avoid giving up on the things you don't like. You can change. If anyone believes in second chances, it's God. Ask Him for a second chance to improve yourself so you will be a good Christian witness in today's society.

❖SCRIPTURE:

"A truthful witness saves lives, but a false witness is deceitful." Proverbs 14:25

REFLECTION:

1) Are you easily influenced by peer pressure? Why or why not?

2) What can you do to avoid the temptation of peer pressure that isn't good for you, such as taking drugs?

CHALLENGE:

Be a good Christian witness by attempting one or more of the following:

* Have a good discussion with an unpopular guy in school.
* Visit an elderly person in a nursing home.
* Sign up for volunteer work in a worthwhile charity.
* Help make sandwiches and meals for the homeless.

A Hero Accepts Himself

Do you have any heroes in your life?

Perhaps some famous people come to mind. Or maybe you know a relative or friend who you really admire, but have you ever thought of yourself as a hero? No joke! You are a hero—a real superstar—here's why. God created you!

Perhaps you think about all the things you *don't* like about yourself—like too many freckles and not enough whiskers. Or perhaps no whiskers at all! Or no girlfriends.

Whatever it is you don't like, ask yourself this question: why are you complaining about God's handiwork?

Maybe you never looked at the situation like this before, but stop and think—meditate—on this fact: God doesn't make trash! Quite the contrary. God gave you special talents, intelligence, and a great personality.

Is it time to change your negative self-talk and self-image?

If so, wear a grin and forget the freckles or lack of whiskers.

Instead, create a strong positive personal image of yourself. Begin thinking of yourself as a real champion, one super dude because you are special and unique.

Why gripe when you can rejoice over your body? It walks, it talks, it runs.

And another thing—your brain is far more brilliant than any computer. Think of how much information you store in your personal database inside your head. It's amazing! Consider how much knowledge you've stored in your brain just from what you have learned at school—algebra formulas, literature, history. You name it.

Realize you're great because God made you one complete and unique individual, different from anyone else.

In other words, celebrate your existence *and* your differences!

❖SCRIPTURE:

"So God created man in His own image . . . God saw all that He had made, and it was very good . . . . " Genesis 1:27,31.

REFLECTION:

1) What do you think of yourself? Are you generally pleased with your image? Or do you waste a lot of time thinking about yourself as a loser? Why or why not?
2) Why is it important to have positive thoughts about yourself?
3) Do you know someone who accepts himself or herself as a hero? If so, how does that person act and react around other people? Why do you know that person has a positive self-image? Is it the things they do or say?

CHALLENGE:

* Quick! Take this mental quiz. Think of how many heroes you have in your life. Okay. Now, did you count yourself? Why or why not?
* Remember, you need to be on your own hero list because God made you special!

To be accepting of others, S.R.
you must first accept yourself

LORD, HELP ME THROUGH THE STORMS OF LIFE.

He stilled the storm to a whisper;

the waves of the sea were hushed.

Psalm 107:29

Is it Cowardly to Cry?

Do you consider crying a cowardly behavior for males?

When was the last time you cried?

In today's society, as I'm sure you are well aware, guys are often expected to be tough. Did it ever occur to you that it's *healthy* to feel emotions like sadness and anger? Have you considered that perhaps males who totally internalize their grief and anger are cowards? At some point, these emotions will surface in less healthy ways than tears.

When Mark was a teen, he figured he shouldn't cry. He thought that as a Christian he needed to be happy all the time to be a positive witness to others.

"I even thought crying was a sin for Christians," he said. "I realize now that's not true."

How right Mark is—it is *not* true!

The Bible doesn't say Christians are a group of people who go around rejoicing about everything all the time. In fact, it's just the opposite. Even Jesus Christ cried! We can take comfort that Jesus Christ experienced sad feelings too—many times. We can't expect to always be happy on earth.

Heaven is the only place described in the Bible as a home where we will be happy, content, and at peace all the time. In fact, that's why Jesus Christ was sent to earth—to tell us the good news.

❖SCRIPTURE:

"There is a time for everything, and a season for every activity under heaven: . . . a time to weep and a time to laugh; a time to mourn and a time to dance . . . " Ecclesiastes 3:1,4

REFLECTION:

1) Do you allow yourself to cry when something bad happens? Why or why not?
2) Do you think Jesus Christ considers crying a weakness?

CHALLENGE:

* Select a Christian friend to talk to—a trusted friend who you can call on when you're depressed or angry and need help, someone who will listen to you, keep your conversation confidential, and not judge you.
* As Christians, you can bind together and support each other in your Christian faith and accept the fact that you're bound to have sad feelings from time to time like everyone else.

WHEN LIFE GIVES YOU A BUM RAP

Do you ever get disappointed?

Of course! Everyone has disappointments. The Bible shows that people suffered adversities since the beginning of time.

Think about Jesus. He suffered all kinds of hardships beginning as a young boy.

Recall the popular Bible story of Jesus when he was twelve years old and in the temple. Luke 2:48-50 says, "When his parents saw him, they were astonished. His mother said to him, 'Son, why have you treated us like this? Your father and I have been anxiously searching for you.' 'Why were you searching for me?' he asked. 'Didn't you know I had to be in my father's house?' But they did not understand what he was saying to them."

His parents' lack of understanding had to be disappointing to Jesus. But look at what happened. Luke 2:51 says, "Then he went down to Nazareth with them and was obedient to them…" Note how He obeyed his parents anyway.

So what are you to do today when you face the disappointment of not making the football team? Or fail that important history test? Or get turned down when you ask a girl for a date?

As a Christian, learn to develop a positive attitude in such situations. So you didn't make the football team. Why not try out for the school play instead?

As for failing the history test—think how you can do better next time. Try studying with a friend. Or try improving your study habits and begin studying well in advance.

Now for the girl turning you down for a date—remember, God made you. You're one terrific person. Go ahead and ask another girl out. She may say yes! Try to avoid focusing on the idea of rejection, but rather consider that this girl lost a great opportunity to get to know you.

Regardless of what problems you face, take comfort in the fact that God is right by your side—always—even during times of disappointment.

❖SCRIPTURE:

"So do not fear, for I am with you; do not be dismayed, for I am your God. I will strengthen you and help you; I will uphold you with my righteous right hand." Isaiah 41:10

REFLECTION:

1) Think of the last time you experienced disappointment. What happened?
2) Think about what to do when faced with disappointment in the future. Plan a positive strategy.
3) Think of Jesus who faced many disappointments while he lived on earth.

CHALLENGE:

* Become involved in a church youth group and develop good Christian friendships. That way you can find comfort in jam sessions with your peers about disappointments.
* Extend yourself to friends with similar values as yours.

Happiness—Check It Out!

Sure, the Bible says we will have disappointments, but it also says we will have good times, too. There will be days when you get that A in history or be chosen for the football team. A girl may accept your invitation to go with you to the movies.

On those days, everything clicks into place. Life is one beautiful miracle. You can see that. What joy! If only life were this easy all the time, you may say to yourself.

Remember this: contentment is God's specialty. He wants mankind to be at peace and enjoy life. His original plan for the Garden of Eden was for man to be in a blissful, content state of mind.

Days of contentment on earth, everyone agrees, are great. Note the ideas below that can bring even more peace in your life, ideas that can give you a high—without drugs. Implement one or more of these ideas into your Christian life and enjoy the natural highs it brings you.

❖SCRIPTURE:

"Is any one of you in trouble? He should pray. Is anyone happy? Let him sing songs of praise." James 5:13

REFLECTION:

1) Check yourself out. Are you content today? Why or why not?
2) What can you do when you're not content?

CHALLENGE:

Hobbies can bring much contentment in people's lives. Check out one or more of these hobby ideas for your life.
* Learn to play an instrument or take vocal music lessons
* Enjoy basketball, soccer, football, or another sport like karate
* Join 4-H, the boy's club, or Boy Scouts

* Do computer work or join a computer club
* Take art or writing lessons
* Learn how to cook
* Ride a horse
* Add your own ideas to this list

Friendship is God's Idea

Meet Max—eighteen years old, handsome, intelligent, and a college freshman. Max liked to be cool, act like he didn't care about anything or anyone.

He caused problems on campus. He told teachers he knew more than they did. Often he neglected to do homework. He presented a tough "I-don't-care" image to his classmates. Sometimes Max dressed in black, including a long coat and hat. Classmates feared he could be a gang member.

Max's teachers found it impossible to make a connection with Max.

So imagine the computer lab teacher's surprise when one day Max announced to some classmates that he didn't know which was most important: power or friends.

"Friends," said one girl.

"Power," said another classmate.

"Max, I think friends are most important. You can be powerful and still lonely," the teacher said.

Max's brown eyes widened. He actually made eye contact with the teacher—something he seldom did with anyone. The teacher had his attention! She would never forget what happened next.

He paused, cleared his throat, and then said, "Hummn. That's interesting. That's something I'm going to have to think about."

Even Max, who tried to play it so cool, so tough, so rebellious, admitted he wasn't sure what to do when it came to the friends vs. power issue.

I hope you have good Christian friends to hang out with on a daily basis. If you don't, ask God for help in finding friends. After all, friendship is his idea! And while you're at it—say a special prayer for Max that he, too, will find good Christian friends.

❖SCRIPTURE:

"Two are better than one, because they have a good return

for their work: If one falls down, his friend can help him up. But pity the man who falls and has no one to help him up!" Ecclesiastes 4: 9, 10

REFLECTION:

1) Do you have friends? Why or why not?
2) What is your personal feeling about friendships?

CHALLENGE:

Try one or more of our suggestions for making friends:
* Attend a youth group and make an effort to talk to some of the kids you don't know.
* Offer to do something kind for one of your peers.
* Invite someone to your home for a jam session or to the beach to go skim boarding.

S.R.

Friendship is God's idea

Promises to Friends

A promise carried out by a friend can be a great blessing. On the other hand, you feel let down if a friend promises you something and then doesn't follow through.

"But that's just human nature," some may say.

Even though there may be truth in that statement, it's important to keep a promise to someone and vice versa. That's one of the ways real friendships are formed.

And, think of God. We can strive to follow God's example. He always keeps his promises! In fact, promises are a dominant theme of the Bible. Matthew 11:28 says, "Come unto me, all ye that labor and are heavy laden, and I will give you rest."

Isaiah 40:29 states, "He gives strength to the weary and increases the power of the weak." And, Isaiah 40:31 boldly affirms, "But they who hope in the Lord shall renew their strength; they will soar on wings like eagles; they will run and not grow weary, they will walk and not be faint."

So, the next time you make a promise to a friend, remember to stick to it. And be blessed with God's abundant grace. He loves promise keepers.

❖SCRIPTURE:

"So when you talk to God and vow to him that you will do something, don't delay in doing it, for God has no pleasure in fools. Keep your promise to him. It is better not to say you'll do something than to say you will and then not do it." Ecclesiastes 5:4 (Living Bible Edition)

REFLECTION:

1) Think about a friend who made you a special promise and kept it. Recall the pleasant memory, reliving the details. Allow God's peace to surround you.
2) Are you keeping your promises you make to friends? If not, why not?

CHALLENGE:
* Today make it a point to promise something good to a friend; make sure it is a promise you will keep—and then carry it out.
* Thank someone who made a promise to you and kept it. Tell that person how much the promise-keeping meant to you.

Is It Okay for Guys to Have Fun?

What is fun?

Perhaps to one person, fun means going to the movies. Someone else may prefer playing basketball. Still another may enjoy reading. Fun means different things to different people.

So, the issue is this: is it okay for Christians to have fun? Certainly—as long as it is clean fun. This means activities that promote health and grows your mind.

Using drugs, reading pornography, viewing sexually-explicit movies are negative behaviors. Our Lord doesn't want us to use drugs that hurt our bodies. (You can read more about the drug issue in the following devotion.) God gave you a sharp mind and will bless your efforts to feed your mind with positive, clean literature and academic subjects.

And, that brings up another issue: having other gods in our lives. When you think about it, most anything good can become our "god" if we allow it. On the other hand, there are lots of fun activities you can do as a Christian teen.

At this point, you may be wondering how to know what the right thing to do is in a certain situation. For assurance, read what God says to us in the following scripture.

❖SCRIPTURE:

"Trust in the Lord with all your heart and lean not on your own understanding: in all your ways acknowledge him, and he will make your paths straight." Proverbs 3:5-6

REFLECTION:

1) Take a look at the Christians you know. Do you think they're having fun with God and living a godly life?
2) Do you think *you* are having fun as a Christian? Why or why not?

CHALLENGE:

Try some of these ideas:
* Start a new hobby
* Read a novel
* Invite a friend over for a pizza or ice cream
* Play some basketball or soccer or go jogging.

What About Drugs?

Take a look at the title. What about drugs? Are they part of your life? Hey man, you may be thinking, don't get on my case. After all, I don't have a problem with drugs. I don't drink that much. I only have a few beers now and then at a party. What's wrong with that? Or perhaps you use marijuana once in awhile. So what? you may say. Everyone's doing it!

Realize the result of drugs is depression, anxiety, panic attacks, and numerous other negative conditions that eventually destroy a person's mind, body, and spirit.

I know some fellows who were convinced that using drugs once in awhile wouldn't hurt them. One of them suffered from severe malnutrition from alcohol use. When he died, he was in diapers and weighed only ninety pounds, even though he was six-feet-four inches tall.

A couple young men I knew were killed in car accidents because they drove while intoxicated. So, don't let anyone fool you when they say, "It's just alcohol." Alcohol is a strong drug. Another boy I knew used drugs, and he committed suicide because of the panic and depression, which are serious side effects of harmful drugs.

Other effects from drug use are: loss of muscle motor control, blurred vision, seizures, breathing problems, coma and, of course, death itself, according to information presented on web site: http://www.health.org. You can see for yourself.

Listen to the advice of one man who is a former drug addict. "Drugs won't do one good thing for you. They'll do lots of bad things but not one good thing." And, think about this: about 19,000 people die from drug-related deaths every year, according to statistics given on the web site of MayoClinic.com

Stop right now and ask yourself: are drugs really worth it? It takes a *man* to answer that question honestly.

❖SCRIPTURE:

"And call upon me in the day of trouble; I will deliver you and you will honor me." Psalms 50:15

REFLECTION:

1) Have you ever been tempted to take drugs? If so, why and what were the circumstances? Did you refrain from the temptation?
2) Have you ever used drugs? If so, why or why not?
3) Do you know of a friend, sibling, or parent whose life has been affected by someone else's alcohol abuse? Might this person be helped by fellowship with Al-Anon or Alateen?

CHALLENGE:

* If you know someone who has a drug problem, take time to say a special prayer for that person.
* If you are a recovering drug addict who has experienced God's forgiveness and know Christ is the answer, tell someone about it today.
* If you think you may have a drug problem, get help now. Call 1-800-821-4357. This number is free of charge, like God's grace. If you or someone you know has an alcohol abuse problem, check out a web page on Alcoholism.about.com. By calling 1-800-234-0420, you can learn more about AA.

> "Who has woe? Who has sorrow?
> Who has strife? Who has complaints?
> Who has needless bruises?
> Who has bloodshot eyes?
> Do not gaze at wine when it is red,
> when it sparkles in the cup, when it goes down smoothly!
> In the end it bites like a snake and poisons like a viper.
> Your eyes shall see strange sights
> and your mind imagine confusing things.
> You will be like one sleeping on the high seas,
> lying on top of the rigging.
> 'They hit me,' you say, 'but I'm not hurt!
> They beat me, but I don't feel it!
> When will I wake up so I can find another drink?'"
>
> Proverbs 23:29-35 (NIV)

Forgive Others—and Yourself

The dictionary defines the word forgive "to give up resentment of or claim to requital or to cease to feel resentment against" someone.

Forgiveness is vital to successful Christian living, but forgiving someone for a wrongdoing is hard to do. It's not easy to throw revenge out the door when a friend says or does something that offends or distresses you.

If you're totally honest with yourself, no doubt there were times when you hurt someone and needed forgiveness.

I've known several young people who confided in their youth pastor in such situations. What a neat idea! Pastors and counselors are often trained to listen and advise in tough times.

The person I've known who practiced forgiveness to the ultimate was a wonderful Christian woman named Susan, who passed away several years ago. When she was living, her only son was murdered by a relative who was later sent to prison for the crime.

"Hatred filled my heart even though I didn't mean to allow that to happen, but it did," Susan said.

One day Susan sat on the edge of her bed and cried out to the Lord. She asked God how he could take her only son.

At that point, Susan said a supernatural spiritualness swept over her, and God silently told her that he had to forgive many people when his only son was killed.

Susan went to the prison and told her son's murderer that she forgave him. Tears streamed down his face. He hugged and thanked her for displaying such Christian warmth.

To be able to forgive is one of the greatest gifts a Christian can give to another person and to himself. So the next time someone hurts you, remember Susan and how she practiced her Christian faith.

❖SCRIPTURE:

"Be kind and compassionate to one another, forgiving each other, just as in Christ God forgave you." Ephesians 4:32

REFLECTION:

1) Think about the last sentence of this reflection and how important you are–unique–made in God's image. You deserve to forgive yourself for your wrongdoings.
2) Also reflect on how God realizes that humans make mistakes, but he's more than willing to forgive us time and time again.

CHALLENGE:

Think about your life. Have you done anything that you haven't forgiven yourself for? Maybe you can think of several things but don't exactly know how to ask the Lord for forgiveness. It's simple. You can pray the Lord's Prayer, which includes asking God to forgive you of all the wrong things you may have done. The prayer can be found in Matthew 6:9-13.

Brag, Brag, Brag!

Meet Bill. As a high school senior, he was intelligent and handsome, but he didn't have many friends. When he began a conversation, Bill noted that everyone drifted away.

"I was always bragging about something or other in my teen years," he explained. "Well, one day I heard our minister say that Proverbs was written for young people, and it was part of the wisdom literature from Israel.

"I'd never read the Bible my parents had given me, but what the minister said really interested me. I wondered what wise sayings Proverbs could possibly say to a cool guy like myself?"

When Bill got home, he was curious. He pulled out his Bible from a drawer, blew off the dust, and began reading. Before long, Bill understood why the book was classified as Biblical wisdom.

"It was like I slowly realized why I didn't have many friends," Bill said. "I never listened to other people. I always wanted to tell my side of the story and, of course, I thought I was always right. Reading Proverbs literally changed my life."

Bill grinned and gave me the following scripture from Proverbs, which especially helped him. I pray it will bless you, too.

❖SCRIPTURE:

"Pride goes before destruction, a haughty spirit before a fall." Proverbs: 16:18

"All the days of the oppressed are wretched, but the cheerful heart has a continual feast." Proverbs 15:15

"Do not boast about tomorrow, for you do not know what a day may bring forth. Let another praise you, and not your own mouth; someone else, and not your own lips." Proverbs 27:1,2

REFLECTION:

1) Do you brag about yourself? Why or why not?
2) Do you have many friends? Why or why not?

3) Have you ever noticed that some people who brag are often the same people who bully or intimidate other kids?

CHALLENGE:

Try our brag-busters listed below the next time you talk to someone:

* Listen to what the other person is saying, instead of thinking about your response. If you have comments, save them until after the person is done talking. Everyone hates to be interrupted.
* Make it a point to give your full attention to a person talking by having direct eye contact.
* Before your conversation ends, give that person a compliment. Think of something you like about the person talking. Words of sincere praise is a great way to begin strong friendships.

Life Can be Such a Puzzle

Mercy! Can't life get complicated?

You may be in a difficult situation right now and don't have the vaguest idea of how to squeeze out of your tangle of webs.

I don't know what your circumstance may be. Perhaps you're dying to ask the cute blonde with drop-dead blue eyes and a terrific personality for a date. If you could only figure out how to go about it.

On top of that, maybe you failed your math test.

Worse yet, your trouble mountain is already sky high when your parents decide to get all over you again about your messy room. Don't they realize they need to cut you some slack? Can't they give you a break?

No wonder you feel trapped!

When you're in such a situation, try giving *yourself* a break. For example, let's go back to the pretty girl you want to ask out. If you panic at the thought of your mission, consider the telephone or e-mail. You may find it easier to ask her for a date over the phone. Perhaps she'll say yes! (If she doesn't, ask another girl who appeals to you.)

As for the math test, learn from the failure. Remember, it's okay to fail, but it's not okay to allow failure to stop you from trying harder next time. It doesn't take a rocket scientist to figure out you must study. For the next test, study to bring your grade up.

As for your messy room, why not get busy and clean it?

Or, if your life is even more perplexing, maybe you've already asked the blonde girl out—and she became pregnant with your baby! What then? Take a look at our challenge below.

Whatever situation you're in—whether it's serious or not-so-serious—remember God is with you. He can help in such situations. Call on Him. No problem is too big for our heavenly Father to handle!

❖SCRIPTURE:

"Trust in the Lord with all your heart and lean not on your

own understanding; in all your ways acknowledge him, and he will make your paths straight." Proverbs 3:5,6

REFLECTION:

1) What can you do to give yourself a break in whatever situation you are in right now?
2) Why are we to trust God when things get tough?

CHALLENGE:

* If you're in an unhappy situation, make a point to talk to a youth minister, a counselor, a parent, or a Christian friend you trust. It's important to talk to someone who won't judge you. Tell that person about your situation and ask for advice. Yes, life can be a complicated puzzle and a daily balancing act.

S.R.
Life can be such a balancing act

Dealing With Change

What do you think of when you hear the word change? Adjust? Adapt? Convert? Reform? Revise? All of these words imply change.

To be a Christian involves many changes. Note our scripture below. Jesus wants us to be like children, to trust him as we do a parent or good friend. No doubt, you've already experienced how sometimes that's really difficult.

Take the case of Kevin. One day a classmate maliciously stepped on some papers Kevin dropped on the bus.

"I've got to admit it was really hard to be a Boy Scout at that moment, to remember my scout pledge, that I was to do good things. I wanted to punch this guy out," Kevin admitted.

But, instead Kevin picked up his torn papers. Imagine his panic when he didn't know if he could get a new copy written before first period when it was due.

"I felt horrible," Kevin continued to explain the incident. "I wondered why something like that has to happen to me."

Being a Christian, Kevin forced himself to think of Jesus Christ for a moment. "He died on the cross for my sins," Kevin said, his brown eyes bright. "So I figured the least I could do is simply redo the homework and forgive the guy for stepping on my work. I felt better then and managed to get my homework turned in on time."

❖SCRIPTURE:

"At that time the disciples came to Jesus and asked, 'Who is the greatest in the kingdom of heaven?' He called a little child and had him stand among them. And he said: 'I tell you the truth, unless you change and become like little children, you will never enter the kingdom of heaven.'" Matthew 18:1-3

REFLECTION:

1) Think of Kevin in the above story. Have you ever encountered a similar situation? If so, how did it turn out?

2) What can you do to change the bad things in your life into good things?

CHALLENGE:

Today memorize the following prayer. It's a popular prayer in 12-step programs.

Lord, grant me the serenity to accept the things I cannot change, courage to change the things I can, and wisdom to know the difference.

After memorizing the prayer, use it the next time you have to change some circumstance in your life. It may involve a big change or a small one. It doesn't matter. The prayer works for any change situation.

Let Me Think

Have you ever longed for some peace and quiet in your life, just so you could think? No doubt you have. Teens have days when all they want to do is be by themselves to think, daydream, meditate, or to reflect—or whatever you want to call it.

There's nothing wrong with that. In fact, it's wonderful and should be encouraged. The Bible tells us in Psalms 4: 4-5 (LBV) to "Stand before the Lord in awe, and do not sin against him. Lie quietly upon your bed in silent meditation. Put your trust in the Lord, and offer him pleasing sacrifices."

That's why you need to set some time aside for yourself daily. Even five or ten minutes a day. So how do you set aside that time?

You simply make up your mind to do it. You may wish to go to your room, close the door, and flop on the bed. There, you can let your mind wander. You may want to close your eyes to block out any distractions.

Les, a teen man, says he learns a lot about God when he is quiet. He said a peace envelopes him during his reflection time and gives him comfort and a natural high—without drugs. Allow Les to serve as your example to develop some calm moments with God. Do that and you will be blessed.

To manage your time accordingly, realize the need for balance in your life. For example, it wouldn't be good to watch television for 24 hours straight. Nor would it be good to exercise for an entire day, nor to lie with your eyes closed daydeaming for twelve hours. Seek balance in your life. Avoid getting trapped into one activity. Take time to do school homework, school activities, household chores, hang out with good Christian friends, and also meditate silently with our Lord and Savior, Jesus Christ.

❖SCRIPTURE:

"But the Lord is in his holy temple: let all the earth be silent before him." Habakkuk 2:20

REFLECTION:

1) Why should Christians take time to be still?
2) Do you take time to be still? Why or why not?

CHALLENGE:

Today flop on your bed and be still for at least ten minutes, and allow yourself to enjoy God's peace. Reflect and listen.

Reflections: Who am I following?

L.Q.

Whoever serves me must follow me;

and where I am, my servant also will be.

John 12:26

A Place and a Time to Daydream

Daydreams are interesting and can be so relaxing. Yet, in today's society, people rush, rush, rush and often don't take time to daydream. What a shame! Yet I, too, am guilty many times of allowing busywork to interfere with the daydreams in my life.

As a society, we need to daydream. Daydreams are important. Daydreaming is a gift God gives us.

So take some time to simply sit in your favorite chair, crash on your bed, or take a walk on the beach. Listen to sounds from wherever you are—like birds singing, a dog barking, or perhaps a child at play.

When we're still—and meditate—so many awesome things can come to us, if we allow ourselves quiet time. For example, we can daydream about the most pleasant thing we've ever experienced. Or we can daydream about our future. Think about where you'd like to be a year from now. Or five years. Or ten years. Consider the blessings in your life. Let peace surround you with happy memories.

Bill, a high schooler, loves to daydream. One of his daydreams actually helped him to win a state competition in the science fair. He dreamed, he acted, and he won.

Every day we use machinery and merchandise that resulted from daydreams. The computer, telephone, and television were results of someone's daydreams, knowledge, and action.

So let your mind wander and enjoy pleasant thoughts.

❖SCRIPTURE:

"Be still, and know that I am God; . . . " Psalm 46:10

REFLECTION:

1) When was the last time you daydreamed and allowed pleasant thoughts to fill your mind?
2) What do you do when not-so-pleasant thoughts invade your mind as you daydream? Anything? Why or why not?

3) What can you do to not dwell on the bad things that happened to you?

CHALLENGE:

* Today, take at least five to fifteen minutes to daydream.
* Be silent and listen.

S.R.

Reflect—Be silent and listen

Deal With the Present—Today

Sure, you tell your parents, you're going to do your homework—but you'll do it later.

Okay, you tell a friend, you'll be glad to help him study algebra—but not today.

Fine, you say to the church youth leader, you'll give a devotional—but not at this meeting.

If the above comments sound like you, realize that everyone procrastinates from time to time. The problem comes when you put things off until later—things that need to be done right away.

That's what happened to Mike. He wanted to achieve good grades when he began college. He really did, but he didn't want to study today, right now, in the present. He'd study tomorrow, he kept telling his friends and himself.

Well, you guessed it. Tomorrow never came. Just when Mike almost flunked out of college, he made a wise decision to study (after a straightforward talk with his father). Not only did he stay in college, but he made the dean's list in the following semesters.

We have choices to make in life. As a student, we have a choice to study. Or not study. The decision is up to us. God gave us a free will and mind. On the other hand, the Bible points out to not put off things that need to be done today. Remember that, and be blessed.

❖SCRIPTURE:

"For he says, 'In the time of my favor I heard you, and in the day of salvation I helped you.' I tell you, now is the time of God's favor, now is the day of salvation." II Corinthians 6:2

REFLECTION:

1) Have you allowed procrastination to become a regular habit in your life?
2) Do you need to do anything today that shouldn't be put off for tomorrow? Is so, get it done—today.

CHALLENGE:

Do something special today for one of our Christian "witness-in-progress" ideas:

* Visit an elderly person in a nursing home.
* If you have siblings, do something special for them like helping with a chore.
* Call a friend and tell him how much you appreciate his friendship.

Research a Future Career

Do you have your career planned? Or did you think about it and then end up not knowing which direction you want your life to go? Maybe you feel like your life is one complicated maze.

That's understandable. It's not easy to choose a career, and yet it's one of the biggest decisions you will make in your life. I heard a minister say that choosing a career doesn't have to be difficult.

"Think about what blesses you," he explained. "Choose a career that stems from things that bless you and brings out your creativity. Chances are good that you'll be happy."

What do you like to do? Perhaps you love music. Or maybe you're great at math. If so, have you ever thought of becoming a math teacher? Or engineer? Or, if you're like I am, you love to write and would like to become a journalist.

Brent loved art and was forever drawing pictures during class. One day his English teacher asked him to bring the picture to her. She was going to toss it into the wastebasket and tell him to keep his mind on English. But when she looked at the picture, a strange thing happened.

"The talent in Brent's drawing was so apparent that I tacked the picture up for display in my classroom," the teacher said, smiling.

Today, Brent is an artist who teaches art and also has one-man showings for his art work in various cities. Brent is a Christian who asked for guidance in his life. Obviously, God gave him his heart's desire in his life. He will do the same for you, if you simply ask—and then listen.

❖SCRIPTURE:

"In his heart a man plans his course, but the Lord determines his steps." Proverbs: 16:9

REFLECTION:

1) Have you ever asked God to give you guidance for your career decision? Why or why not?

2) Take a moment to reflect on some things people compliment you for doing or being. Then see if your future work may be found in any of the things you obviously do well.

CHALLENGE:

Think about your future today by doing one or more of the following:
* Talk to a teacher and your parents about the careers available to you.
* Ask your friends if they've thought about their careers.
* Go to the library and check out some books on career planning.
* Study college catalogs to see what's available in the different degrees offered.

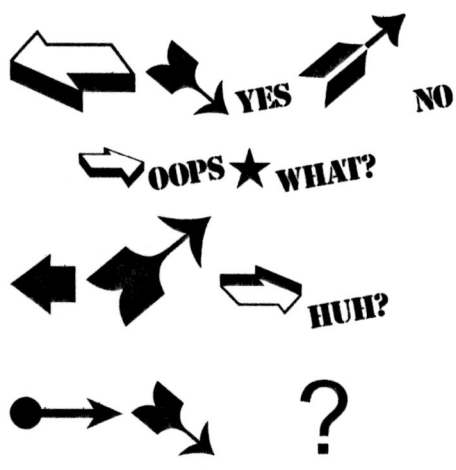

Give Yourself a Break

Trent, a senior in high school, never gave himself a break. He'd go to football practice early in the morning, then to school, then to work at a fast-food restaurant after school.

"I never had time to study because I was so busy doing extracurricular activities," he said.

Soon his teachers noticed his grades dropping. So did Trent's parents. Trent's parents and teachers reminded him the same thing: extracurricular activities are a great way to try new things and accomplish goals, but there are only so many hours in the day.

They suggested Trent drop a couple extracurricular activities and work less hours at the restaurant. That way he could get his homework done.

Trent wasn't wild about the idea, but he did follow their suggestions. Weeks later he felt much less stress and more energy.

"I couldn't believe what a difference those changes made," Trent grinned. "I'm not only getting good grades, but I actually have time to spend with the guys once in awhile or go on a date. Sometimes I just like to sprawl on our backyard hammock and listen to the sounds of nature. My life is so cool now."

Not only is Trent's life cool, but he's living the way Jesus Christ intended. Take a look at the following scripture; you too can have a "cool" life like Trent.

❖SCRIPTURE:

"Come to me, all you who are weary and burdened, and I will give you rest. Take my yoke upon you and learn from me, for I am gentle and humble in heart, and you will find rest for your souls. For my yoke is easy and my burden is light." Matthew 11:28-30

REFLECTION:

1) Are you giving yourself a break—some kind of treat—every day in our busy world? Why or why not?

2) Can Christ help with the stress and anxiety in your life?

CHALLENGE:

Try one of our stress busters:
* List the things you have to do today. What, if anything, could be eliminated? Be honest because, in all probability, there's a thing or two that may not have to be done today.
* Watch a video that you've been wanting to see.
* Go for a relaxing walk in your neighborhood.
* Do something kind for someone else.
* If you don't have time for a regular date, invite a girl out for a soda pop and simply visit for an hour.

What Makes a Guy Good-Looking Anyway?

Stop and think for a moment. What really makes a guy handsome (especially to girls)? Being tall? Trim build? Or heavier and muscular? Dark hair? Blonde hair? Red hair? How about the eye color? Do girls like blue eyes best? Or green eyes? Or brown?

If you like a Christian girl, chances are she'll be much more interested about what kind of a person you are inside—what makes you tick and what your values are rather than being concerned about your physical appearance.

Think about your friends. Are they interested in their outer appearance rather than inner qualities? If so, you may want to examine your choice of friends. As a Christian, it's important to have good friends who are more concerned about their character than they are about how they look on the outside.

So don't get hung up on your outward appearance. Develop your inner qualities, like a good sense of humor, ambition, and integrity. Strive for a positive outlook on life. Learn to be a good conversationalist. If a girl is most interested in your outward appearance, perhaps some other girl will have more depth. Christ looks at your inner qualities.

❖SCRIPTURE:

"Your beauty should not come from outward adornment, such as . . . wearing of gold jewelry and fine clothes. Instead, it should be that of your inner self, the unfading beauty of a gentle and quiet spirit, which is of great worth in God's sight." I Peter 3:3,4

REFLECTION:

1) Are you spending too much time being concerned about your outward appearance?
2) If your answer is yes, what can you do to change?

CHALLENGE:

* Go to your computer and list all the good things about your inner self—like being kind to others, your positive qualities, and your character.
* After you write the list, print it out, read and reread it, and then feel good about yourself. Place it somewhere so you can view it whenever you like. The list can be a great mood lifter for those blue days.

What's the Big Deal with Self-Esteem?

Some schools today offer courses and programs that focus on self-esteem. In some areas these courses have become quite popular. And it's easy to see why.

Superintendents and other school officials often report that after attending self-esteem programs, kids do much better in school academically, as well as socially. Often they have fewer problems at home and with peers than the students who don't like themselves or pay no attention to their self-esteem.

If you have a high self-esteem—in other words if you really like the person you see in the mirror—chances are good that you'll be able to accomplish a lot in your life. If you think little of yourself, your negative self-concept will likely damage your ability to accomplish your dreams. Mental institutions and prisons are filled with people suffering from low self-esteem.

When you think about it, isn't that logical? If you don't have any good thoughts about yourself, how can you reach out in faith and develop a Christian life-style and worthwhile friendships that produce good things? The answer is simple: you really can't. At least, that's what mental health and other professionals say.

So what can you do, as a Christian, to think more highly of yourself? We're not talking conceit here. Look at it this way. God made you and He specializes in quality. After all, God doesn't make junk! Concentrate on that today and feel your self-esteem rise. Think about what you can do for others.

❖SCRIPTURE:

"Keep on loving each other as brothers. Do not forget to entertain strangers, for by so doing some people have entertained angels without know it." Hebrews 13:1-2

REFLECTION:

1) It's important to have a healthy self-esteem. Why?
2) What can you do personally to raise your self-esteem?

CHALLENGE:

Volunteer work has proved to raise people's self-esteem. So volunteer for some worthwhile project. You could:

* Tutor kids having trouble in one of your best subjects—whether it be math, English, science, or a sport.
* Volunteer to help prepare sandwiches for the homeless or for families in a homeless shelter.
* Volunteer to clean your room or prepare dinner to help out a parent or younger sibling.
* Take care of the family pet
* Help build a home with a church group or with Habitat for Humanity.

Attracting Girls

Most teen males want to attract girls. But many guys wonder how that miracle can be accomplished. You probably are no exception.

Good news! Different girls are attracted to different types of boys. Thank God, or wouldn't it be a tough world? So, probably the best thing to do is be yourself. And don't be shy.

Go ahead and ask that blonde or redhead or brunette to a movie, or to a sporting event at school, or a church youth group activity, or for ice cream. She just may say yes.

"But I'll just die if she turns me down," you may think.

Don't let rejection get to you. There's always another girl nearby to ask. Go to your church youth group regularly and visit with some girls there. That's a great place to meet girls. Cultivate some casual friendships there and learn how to talk and effectively listen to other people.

Group dating is popular and is one way to get to know girls in a nonthreatening and ideal way.

And, by all means, pray about it. God cares about your date life.

❖SCRIPTURE:

"Do not be anxious about anything, but in everything, by prayer and petition, with thanksgiving, present your requests to God." Philippians 4:5-6

REFLECTION:

1) Take a notebook and jot down some activities you could do on a date that would be above reproach.
2) Do you think God cares about your date life? Why or why not?

CHALLENGE:

* Sometime today pray a short prayer asking God for guidance in all areas of your life.
* Think about what qualities you admire in a person.
* Figure out your own values so you can do a better job of choosing people with whom you would like to develop friendships.

S.R.

Cultivate some casual friendships

LOVE AND MONEY—DO THEY MIX?

Do you realize you don't have to spend a lot of money to go on a fun date? That is if you've selected a Christian girl who understands that money isn't everything.

Take Richard and Mary. As college freshmen, neither had much spending money. So when they started dating, Richard began to feel like he should spend some money on Mary, but he simply couldn't afford it. Coming from a large family, he had several siblings in school.

So Richard often took Mary on a date to the library. Or out for a cup of coffee and dessert. Sometimes they went for long walks. Did Mary mind? Not at all!

"I really like Richard," she told her friends in the dorm. "We do such fun stuff together. We talk a lot, and he's a neat friend. I'm getting an opportunity to really know him and what's important to him."

Imagine Richard's surprise when Mary told him how much she enjoyed being with him. Today the couple is happily married and can afford to go to an expensive restaurant now and then, or on a weekend trip to a nearby city. Both say that's not what's important, that their relationship never did and never has centered on money. And isn't that great?

If a girl asks you to spend a lot of money on her or wants to know what kind of car you or your parents drive, is she really the girl for you? It's something to think about.

❖SCRIPTURE:

"People who want to get rich fall into temptation and a trap and into many foolish and harmful desires that plunge men into ruin and destruction. For the love of money is a root of all kinds of evil. Some people, eager for money, have wandered from the faith and pierced themselves with many griefs." I Timothy 6:9-10

REFLECTION:

1) Should money be important in your date life? Why or why not?

2) Can you see how the love of money creates problems?

CHALLENGE:

Try one of our ideas for a free date:
* Go to a youth group at the church of your choice.
* Take a hike and enjoy God's handiwork.
* Plan a game night and invite another couple to play monopoly or some other game.

WHAT ABOUT SEX?

Let's talk about girls and sexual behavior.

If your feelings for the opposite sex embarrass you, take comfort in the fact the feelings are normal. God created sex. So what do you do about it? you wonder. Go ahead and have premarital sex? After all, everyone's doing it. So what difference would it make?

A lot.

Craig is in his teens and wondered about those same questions. After much sex education and prayer, he realized that sexual desire does not disappear when a boy makes a decision not to have sex before marriage, but he decided which road he would take during his teen years.

"I've made a decision about something that I'm really happy about," he told me one day. "I've decided not to have premarital sex. I mean it's just not worth it. I could end up with AIDS or one of the other 47 sexually-transmitted diseases. Or I could get a girl pregnant. Then I'd probably become a poverty-stricken teen father who would have to quit school to work full time in order to support a kid. Or my girlfriend might decide on an abortion, which would be heart breaking. Or she may give the baby up for adoption, and I'd never get to know the child. Or I might be pressured into marrying someone I don't want to marry. I'm going to save myself for my future wife." I marveled at this Christian teen. What a courageous and wise stand to make in today's society!

Maybe you agree that Craig's decision is wise, but you've already had sexual intercourse with a girl. Or girls. Well, examine God's promises. If you ask for his forgiveness with a contrite heart, God is always willing to forgive your past, and he's interested in your future. It's never too late to ask for God's help.

Every teen needs to be acutely aware of the impact alcohol and drugs have on lowering one's inhibitions. Intelligent and caring teens will avoid partaking of mind-altering drugs (including alcohol). If you are dating a girl who participates in this type of activity, it is best to run the other way.

Although temptation is ever present, a boy who really cares about himself and about a girl will want the best for her and encourage her to save herself for her future husband.

❖SCRIPTURE:

"My son, pay attention to my wisdom, listen well to my words of insight, that you may maintain discretion and your lips may preserve knowledge. For the lips of an adulteress drip honey, and her speech is smoother than oil; but in the end she is bitter as gall, sharp as a double-edged sword. Her feet go down to death; her steps lead straight to the grave. She gives no thought to the way of life; her paths are crooked, but she knows it not." Proverbs 5:1-6.

REFLECTION:

1) Is it normal for you to be obsessed with girls at times?
2) What does the Bible tell you to do when it comes to girls and sex?

CHALLENGE:

* Participate in group dates and create opportunities to be with your girlfriend in situations where sexual pressure is limited.
* Look for ways to show you care about your girlfriend that does not rely on physical expression.

Say a simple prayer today. Ask God to help you with your sexual feelings, to guide you and give you strength to say no to temptation when it comes to sexual desires.

What About Abortion?

On her first day of teaching, Danielle was confronted by Brittany, a distraught teen student who burst into her office and cried, "I don't know what to do!" Tears poured down Brittany's face.

"What is it?" Danielle, a caring Christian, inquired.

"I'm pregnant and my steady boyfriend and I only had intercourse one time! How could that happen?"

"Girls are very fertile in their growing-up years," Danielle said softly in understanding.

Thank God, Brittany's story turned into a happy one. Even though she was pregnant, her steady boyfriend wanted to marry her and help raise their child, since both deeply loved each other. So they got married and had a beautiful baby.

Even though the above scenario turned out quite well, Brittany and her husband want others to know teenage parenthood is tough. There are dirty diapers, feedings, bathing, crying at night, and numerous other things to do to care for a baby. And there are also financial worries.

Now meet Lauren. She had five abortions and three children. When her friend asked why she got the abortions and yet had children, Lauren said, "Those pregnancies just weren't at the right time."

In other words, Lauren used abortions as birth control. Would you want your wife to do that?

What about those of you who made a girl pregnant, and she had an abortion. Now you regret the decision. Is God going to punish you? According to the Bible, God forgives everything if you are truly sorry and ask for forgiveness. What a miracle God's love and compassion is to listen to the likes of us.

Or if you are in the unfortunate situation in which a girl is pregnant with your child, you feel you have nobody with whom you can discuss this matter, and you have no idea what to do, you may want to consider calling 1-800-848-LOVE. This is a crisis line for people who may want to consider adoption.

❖SCRIPTURE:

"For God so loved the world that he gave his one and only Son, that whoever believes in him shall not perish but have eternal life. For God did not send his Son into the world to condemn the world, but to save the world through him." John 3:16-17

REFLECTION:

1) What do you think about Brittany?
2) What do you think about Lauren? As Christians, are we to judge them?

CHALLENGE:

Talk to your parents or an older sibling about questions and ethical solutions to problems. If there is not a family member who is willing and able to discuss these issues with you, seek out a Christian youth worker, clergy person, or school nurse to answer some questions you have.

Since abortion is such a serious issue, you can be a great Christian witness to other guys by not going all the way with a girl until you marry. And, if you're sexually active already, you can stop—with God's help—and wait to have further sexual relations until you find that Christian girl of your dreams who you want to marry.

What About Homosexuality?

AIDS continues to spread in teenage men who participate in homosexual activities, according to information presented on the web site: http://www.aegis.com.

Even though homosexuality, like abortion, is a controversial issue in today's society, it's nothing new. St. Paul said a lot about this subject. In this time in history, we cannot look at the news without seeing the words "gay marriage" and "civil unions."

As you know, some people argue that homosexuals are born with homosexual tendencies and others argue that people are homosexual because they made a decision to become a homosexual for a variety of reasons. There is so much confusion over this issue that sometimes Christians neglect the basic part of the issue: Is it okay to be homosexual? Or does God punish homosexuals? Is it acceptable to be tolerant or kind to homosexuals?

Chances are very good that most teens who read this book are aware of a boy or boys in his school who he suspects or knows is gay. How is this person treated? Do his classmates isolate him and chastise him? Do they tease him and avoid him?

It may even be a temptation to look down on classmates who are kind or respectful to those who are different from the other students, whether it be racial differences, ethnic or religious differences, physical or mental disabilities, or homosexuality.

As Christians, realize we're not to judge anyone. The Bible spells that out. We are to treat each human being with respect, even though we may disagree with his behavior or choices. But, at the same time, read the scripture below: I Corinthians 6:9-11.

❖SCRIPTURE:

"If I say, 'My foot slips,' Your mercy, Oh Lord, will hold me up. In the multitude of my anxieties within me, Your comforts delight my soul. (Psalm 94:18-19 NKJV)

REFLECTION:

1) Do you consider yourself homosexual? Why or why not?

2) What does God want you to be when it comes to sexuality?

CHALLENGE:

* Do not judge the homosexual but show your compassion in the Christian faith. If the homosexual wants help, there are numerous phone numbers of hot lines available. Begin by calling 1-800-421-4211. This is the number of the National Mental Health Association. They have professionals to aid anyone in whatever problem they are facing.
* Ask a mature adult Christian friend to give you advice if you're ever faced with this situation.
* If you are a homosexual, research what the Bible says about this life-style. And pray about your life, knowing God cares for you.
* Consider how you interact with those who are different from you. As a Christian, examine your actions.

Running Away From Home

Every year between 1.3 and 2.8 million teens run away from home and end up on the streets, according to recent statistics from the National Runaway Switchboard. One out of every seven kids will flee from home sometime before they reach eighteen years of age, the statistics further indicate. Whatever problem the teen is facing in his situation can vary from mild to serious.

On the serious side, perhaps you have a drug problem and you're fed up with your parents being on your case all the time. Or, on the less serious side, maybe you're just fed up with living at home and dealing with parents and siblings in general. Or, perhaps you live in a single-parent household. Or, maybe you've got a stepparent with whom you must deal. Whatever the situation, you figure you deserve better than the treatment you're presently receiving. If you are being abused by a parent or family member, you DO deserve better! In that case, seek help from a professional—immediately.

You may feel that you've grown up. You think you'd be better off on your own. Stop! Would you *really*?

If you've already run away from home or are thinking about it, consider this. Where will you go? What will you do? Do you have any money? Or will you end up on the streets? Be aware that teens on the streets often end up in the morgue. Every year about 5,000 runaways die from either assault, illness or suicide, according to the National Runaway Switchboard.

Surely, there's a better way to handle things. Like what? you may wonder. For starters, try talking to a teacher or youth minister. Be honest and level with them. A professional Christian with counseling skills can help you find the right direction—the one Jesus Christ wants for you. That way you can't go wrong! Isn't that something worth thinking about—and doing?

Sure, that may be okay for some guys, you may be thinking, but I'm too embarrassed to talk to anyone face to face. If that's the case, try this nonprofit organization for help. What do you have to lose? The switchboard, organized in 1974, has a caring and professional staff who reaches out to teens in your situation. Tell them your problems, which will be held strictly confidential, by calling 1-800-621-4000. If you don't feel like using the phone, go to their web site: www.nrscrisisline.org. Or reach out to some other nonprofit organization that can help. There are many similar organizations that can help teen runaways.

❖SCRIPTURE:

"Do not be anxious about anything, but in everything, by prayer and petition, with thanksgiving, present your requests to God. And the peace of God, which transcends all understanding, will guard your hearts and your minds in Christ Jesus." Philippians 4:6-7

REFLECTION:

1) What can you do when you're fed up with your parent(s)?
2) Do your friends have problems with their parent(s) too?
3) Are you being considerate of your parents?

CHALLENGE:

* Take a look at your home situation and pray about it today. Our Lord and Savior is standing by you, ready to help and guide you if you just ask.
* Suggest to a youth minister to have a discussion group about parents that would include Christian coping mechanisms for what you can do when you get fed up with your home life.
* If there are serious issues of abuse, seek help from a professional counselor or organization.

MAKING DEMANDS ON PARENTS

"But Dad, I've *got* to have the car Saturday night! That's all there is to it!"

"But Mom, you just don't understand! I need some money to buy a computer game, and I want it *now*!"

If you can identify with either (or both) of the demands made above, take time out. Are you making demands on your parents?

Professional counselors say the demands above aren't even reasonable. So, if you're getting your way all the time when you demand something, your parents aren't even doing you a favor. In the real world, people don't like it when others dictate and command someone to do something.

Perhaps it is your job to attempt to get what you want from your parents. Perhaps you excel at this task. It is the parents' responsibility, however, to provide boundaries for their children. A loving parent provides boundaries that are reasonable and keeps their child safe. Although no one likes being told "no," it is important for each of us to learn how to take "no" for an answer.

As a teen, learning this skill pays off later when attending college or working in the corporate world or learning how to function in society as a responsible adult.

As Christians, we're not suppose to make demands. Proverbs 18:1-2 says, "An unfriendly man pursues selfish ends; he defies all sound judgment. A fool finds no pleasure in understanding but delights in airing his own opinions."

❖SCRIPTURE:

"A son who mistreats his father or mother is a public disgrace." Proverbs 19:26 (Living Bible Edition)

REFLECTION:

1) Do you make it a point to listen to your parents? Why or why not?

2) Can you recall a time when you *demanded* something from one of your parents? If so, what happened?

3) Do you remember a situation where you listened grudgingly and honored a boundary set by your parents? Did it so happen that there was a somewhat positive outcome?

CHALLENGE:

* Make a list of your recent demands. Which ones are NEEDS? Which demands are selfish? Discuss the list with your parents.

When Your Parents Divorce

If your parents are divorced, chances are you think it's not fair. Why did it have to happen to your family? you may wonder. If only they'd worked things out, figured some way to get along! That way you wouldn't have to face this whole mess.

Well, you know what?

It's *not* fair.

But here's something to think about. I Peter 5:12 says, "Beloved, do not think it strange concerning the fiery trial which is to try you, as though some strange thing happened to you;…"

Life on this earth will not be fair in the years ahead either. The Bible tells us that. Life in heaven, however, is a totally different story. Just think. In heaven, there won't be divorces, deaths, sickness, or anything else that causes pain.

Even so, I'm sure that seems hard to believe at times. But, as Christians, we are assured that our sorrows on this earth won't last forever. Eventually we will live in peace.

So what do you do right now? Sure, heaven sounds great, but that doesn't help you at this time. Perhaps your parents are even fighting over who gets you on Thanksgiving or Christmas. You may even feel like you're caught in the middle—part of you goes to your father and part of you to your mother.

No doubt about it. Divorce is tough for every family member. So try to understand from a Christian perspective. Things will get better.

Take Greg. He's a college student whose parents divorced when he was in high school. He said at first he thought he'd always be angry about the situation. Now, after time, the anger has subsided. He believes that's due to God's healing process.

❖SCRIPTURE:

"He who gets wisdom loves his own soul; he who cherishes understanding prospers." Proverbs 19:8

"Love forgets mistakes; nagging about them parts the best of friends." Proverbs 17:9 (Living Bible Edition)

"He who gets wisdom loves his own soul; he who cherishes understanding prospers." Proverbs 19:8

REFLECTION:

1) What can you do, as a son, to help your parents in *your* difficult times?
2) Would Jesus Christ want you to treat your parents differently since they are divorced? Explain your feelings.

CHALLENGE:

Talk to a youth minister or another Christian adult you trust about how your parent's divorce is affecting you. Be honest. If you're not, you will be robbing yourself from developing some valuable coping skills for this difficult time in your life.

How About a Stepparent?

Meet Jerald. He didn't want a stepfather. Ever! But, as you know, guys can't tell parents what to do.

So Jerald's mother married the man who Jerald classified as a jerk the moment he met him.

"I didn't think I'd ever get used to the idea of my mother with another man," Jerald said. "I wanted her and my father to get back together, but that's not what my parents wanted to do."

Jerald had a hard time. He compared his new stepfather with his natural father. "They were so different. My dad always wore colorful shirts while my stepfather wears nothing but white shirts."

Jerald admits that over time his list of the things he didn't like about his stepfather grew and grew. He didn't like the way his stepfather looked. He also didn't like the occasional meals he cooked. Every time his stepfather tried to give Jerald useful advice—like suggesting he wear a coat when it's freezing outside, Jerald felt totally irritated.

Finally, Jerald's mother arranged to take Jerald out to eat pizza just so the two of them could talk.

"Why can't you be reasonable about Anthony?" his mother wanted to know.

"I just don't like him," was Jerald's quick reply.

The meal wasn't a pleasant one. Jerald couldn't think of one good thing about his stepfather.

"Why did you ever divorce dad in the first place?" he wanted to know.

What happened next surprised Jerald. In a soft voice, his mother answered, "He was having an affair with another woman."

Even though Jerald knew those facts, suddenly it hit him. The reasons for the divorce were valid, he realized. Besides, the more he thought about it, his stepfather never got drunk, and he never beat him up, like his natural father had done a couple times.

Over the next few months, Jerald had more heart-to-heart talks with his mother. She was right. His stepfather was a caring and Christian man who only wanted the best for Jerald.

"It's not easy to be a stepparent," she told Jerald. "Please try to understand."

Jerald did exactly that. He prayed about it, too. Today Jerald is close to his stepfather. The two go fishing together, to the movies, and football games.

"I'm really glad I got over my hateful feelings for my stepdad. He's a cool guy. It took me a long time to realize that."

❖SCRIPTURE:

"A fool thinks he needs no advice, but a wise man listens to others." Proverbs 12:15 (The Living Bible Edition)

REFLECTION:

1) What would you do in Jerald's place? Would you listen to your mother or continue to be negative about your stepparent? Why or why not?
2) What does the Bible say about divorce? Are we to judge the divorced person?

CHALLENGE:

* Make it a point today to write down all the good things about your parents and/or stepparents. Show them the list.

When a Parent Dies

Matthew never expected his father to die when he was in high school. After all, his father was in good health.

So what happened?

His father was 37 years old when one day he rose out of bed and fell to the floor unconscious. His mother called Matthew and his siblings for help after she dialed 911. The emergency 911 team came quickly, but it was too late.

Later, the family doctor told Mrs. Matthews that her husband had a massive coronary.

Matthew still remembers the grief in his mother's voice when she told the doctor, "But that can't be! He never had heart problems."

The doctor shook his head. "I'm very sorry. Sometimes this happens." The doctor laid his hand on Matthew's shoulder. "How are you doing?"

Feeling his chin trembling, Matthew nodded. He was lost for words. His father and he always went fishing together. Often Matthew played football with his dad and his two younger sisters. Sometimes just he and his dad went out for pizza for a man-to-man talk, which Matthew enjoyed so much.

Now what? Matthew wondered. Where will I go from here? Where was God anyway? Why did my very own father have to die?

"The family was so sad," Matthew recalled. "None of us knew what to do."

Even so, their mother decided they would keep going to church. She even arranged for family counseling with their minister.

"At first I didn't want to go to a minister," Matthew admitted. "I felt totally embarrassed that I needed help. My minister finally got it through my head that everyone needs help in this world. It's nothing to be ashamed of."

Now, a year later, Matthew isn't nearly so sad. In fact, sometimes he actually finds great comfort in thinking about his father and what a neat person he was. Matthew's minister said that's a sign of the healing God gives us after we've mourned for a loved one.

❖SCRIPTURE:

"Blessed are those who mourn, for they shall be comforted." Matthew 5:4

REFLECTION:

1) What can we do when a loved one dies?
2) Do you believe God will comfort you when you grieve for a loved one? Why or why not?

CHALLENGE:

* If you know someone who lost a parent, reach out to that person in Christian love and sympathy by visiting with him. If you don't know what to say, don't worry. Just being in the grieving person's presence will help.
* If you already experienced losing a parent, call on a youth leader in a church to help you during the grieving process that will lead to healing.

L.Q.

**REACH FOR THE SUN
STAND BY THE SEA
HELP ME TO BLOSSOM
TO BEAR FRUIT FOR THEE.**

But the fruit of the Spirit is love, joy, peace, patience, kindness, goodness, faithfulness.

Galatians 5:22

PATIENCE—WHAT'S THAT?

The Bible has a lot to say about patience. And with good reason. It's fun to be with people who are patient. Take a look at how the word patience is used in the following scripture:

Proverbs 25:15 states, "Through patience a ruler can be persuaded, and a gentle tongue can break a bone."

Colossians 1:11 says, "…being strengthened with all power according to his glorious might so that you may have great endurance and patience, and joyful giving thanks to the Father, who has qualified you to share in the inheritance of the saints in the kingdom of light."

It's interesting to observe how frequently patience is brought up in Scripture. In I Corinthians 13:4-6 we are told, "Love is patient, love is kind. It does not envy, it does not boast, it is not proud. It is not rude, it is not self-seeking. It is not easily answered, it keeps no record of wrongs." Perhaps Paul lists patience as the first ingredient of love because it is the most challenging task for us to accomplish!

Now look at the following verses in James 5:7-8: "Be patient, then, brothers, until the Lord's coming. See how the farmer waits for the land to yield its valuable crop and how patient he is for the autumn and spring gains. You, too, be patient and stand firm…"

As Christians, every one of us would be wise to practice patience in our daily living. But, as I'm sure you know, it's not always easy to be patient. You may find yourself gritting your teeth when you have to wait for your brother or sister to get ready for church—again! Or when your dad insists you mow the yard—today! Or your mother wants you to clean your room—pronto!

The good news is we can practice patience in our daily lives until it becomes a habit. How? Simply follow our challenges that feature things requiring patience.

❖SCRIPTURE:

"…He is patient with you, not wanting anyone to perish, but everyone to come to repentance." 2 Peter 3:9

REFLECTION:

1) Would you describe yourself basically as a patient or impatient person?
2) Recall a time when you weren't patient. What happened?
3) Now think of another time when you *were* patient. What happened then?
4) Are you patient with your parents and siblings?

CHALLENGES:

* Take time to be patient with the next person who seems impatient with you.
* If you have a friend who's particularly patient, call and thank him for his kindness.
* Jot the scriptures on note cards and review them before you go to bed tonight. Then say a prayer, asking God to grant you patience in your daily Christian living.

Stress is so Stressful!

Do you ever get stressed out of your skull? Those were the words fourteen-year-old Calvin used when he described a hectic time he had at school one day.

"Everything piled up," Calvin began to explain to his friend Daryl on their way home. "It was like every teacher was out to get me. My math teacher gave a long assignment, my history teacher assigned a test, and I had no idea what my English teacher was talking about today. Wish I were you! You're so organized!"

Daryl laughed. "Not really. It probably just looks that way to you. I've got my 'humongous' headache days, too."

"As for headaches, I've got one right now," Calvin groaned.

The first thing Daryl suggested to Calvin was to set priorities.

"How do I do that?" Calvin wanted to know.

"Want me to explain today's English class?" Daryl said.

Calvin nodded. "Super. It's worth a try."

So, an hour later and after help from Daryl, Calvin actually understood the English class lecture. After dinner, Calvin and Daryl got together for a cola and a think-tank session on history. After Daryl left, Calvin whizzed through his math assignment before going to bed. He had no problems with the assignment since Daryl accurately describes Calvin as a "math genius."

When Calvin went to bed, he noticed for the first time that his headache vanished hours ago. Isn't it a good feeling when you've done your homework? Take pride in your good accomplishments. God does. Remember, Jesus faced lots of stresses in his life, too. So, by all means, tell Jesus about the stress in your life. He can help you cope through those extra stressful days.

❖SCRIPTURE:

"A righteous man may have many troubles, but the Lord delivers him from them all . . ." Psalm 34:19.

REFLECTION:

1) When was the last time you were really stressed? What did you do about it?
2) What don't you like about stress?
3) Can there be any positive effects of stress?

CHALLENGES:

We've complied a list of stress-busters for you. Try one or more of them one day.
* Take a fifteen-minute jog and enjoy God's creation.
* Go roller skating or roller blading.
* Call a friend over for a talk session.
* Sit and listen to some soothing music.
* Try to figure out the reasons for your stress and consider ways to cope with the problem(s) instead of digging yourself deeper and deeper into that stressful place.

S.R.

Sometimes we just dig ourselves deeper and deeper

When a Friend Dies

Have you ever had a friend die?

Sixteen-year-old Malissa did. In fact, she had four close teen friends, two boys and two girls, who were killed in a car accident. The teens had been drinking, including the driver.

When Malissa heard the news, she was horrified.

"Nothing was the same after that," she recalled. "I went around in a daze for several months. I was so sad and depressed."

More months passed.

A year later, Malissa is still mourning the loss of her friends, but through God's help she is continuing on with her life as a Christian and is making some wise choices. For example, about a month ago, some friends invited her to a party.

"Is there going to be alcohol there?" she wanted to know.

The kids said yes.

"Then the only way I'll go is if I can be the designated driver. I won't drink."

"Hey, I'm not letting you or anyone else drive my new car," Bill said.

"Well, will you be drinking?" Malissa wanted to know.

"Yes," Bill admitted.

"Then I'm not going to the party." Malissa was firm.

"Why not?" one girl wanted to know.

"Yeah, why not?" another guy asked.

"Because I don't want to die! Alcohol kills! I don't want to drink again," Malissa said.

And that's so true. Alcohol and other drugs are destructive. Remember that. Let Malissa be your shining testimony when you're asked to go to a party where alcohol will be served.

❖SCRIPTURE:

"Cast your cares on the Lord and he will sustain you; he will never let the righteous fall." Psalms 55:22

REFLECTION:

1) Do you understand why alcohol now frightens Malissa? Why or why not?
2) What would you have done if you had been in Malissa's place? Why or why not?

CHALLENGE:

* If you know someone who lost a good friend, go to that person and tell him or her that you're sorry for their loss.
* If you've lost a great friend, comfort yourself by reading the entire chapter of Psalm 55.

FEELING LEFT OUT

Do you ever feel left out?

Like civilization has a purpose, but you don't?

Or perhaps you faced personal rejection that you're finding difficult. Perhaps you weren't selected for this year's football team or you weren't chosen to play the tuba in band. Maybe you didn't get the part you wanted in the school play.

On the other hand, perhaps everything that surrounds you appears fine, but you feel down anyway. You're depressed, lonely, even panicky at times.

These depressive feelings hit teen guys, too. It doesn't just happen to girls, like society would sometimes have us believe.

On your down days, the good news is you can turn to a source that offers comfort, hope, blessing—the Holy Bible. It's not a coincidence that the Bible continues to be a best-seller. It's because people find hope in our Lord and Savior, Jesus Christ. We can do the same. How fortunate we are that we have a record of Jesus' life and how He cares for us!

Now find comfort, peace, and joy in the following scripture, reflection, and challenge selected just for you.

❖SCRIPTURE:

"Do not be anxious about anything, but in everything, by prayer and petition, with thanksgiving, present your requests to God. And the peace of God, which transcends all understanding, will guard your hearts and your minds in Christ Jesus." Philippians 4:6-7

REFLECTION:

1) Think about the times you are lonely, or frightened, or depressed. What have you done about such feelings? And why?
2) Is it okay for Christians to have feelings of depression?

CHALLENGE:

* Take a sheet of paper and jot down some things—fun and clean Christian-approved things—that make you happy. Now, look at the sheet and see if you've treated yourself lately. If you haven't for some time, study the list and do something positive on your list today.
* Life can be confusing and sometimes lonely. Consider some activities that you can enjoy with a friend or two—or even by yourself.

S.R.

Life can be confusing and lonely.

Joining Cults

Wanna fit in with the crowd? Feel like you're worth something? Be one cool dude?

Most teens will answer yes to the above questions. The questions sound innocent. And they are—to a certain extent. But the questions can also turn your life upside down if you make some wrong choices such as joining a violent gang—or getting involved with a prejudiced hate group who is against a certain race of people—or becoming a member of a satanic cult.

Sean Sellers, a former satanic cult member, conducted cult activity that landed him in the Oklahoma State Penitentiary. He confessed he killed his parents when he was a teenager. He was put on death row and executed. Before his death, he claimed to have a born-again experience and worshiped only God. Maybe Sean realized that cult activity doesn't bring power, that victory is found in Jesus Christ.

Before you join any group, take a close inventory. Look at the leader. Is he or she a Christian? What is the group's purpose or mission? What activities and projects do they participate in? What contribution, if any, are they giving to society?

And, last but not least, ask yourself if Jesus Christ would approve of such a group. If Christ himself wouldn't approve of the group, why join it?

❖SCRIPTURE:

"A righteous man is cautious in friendship, but the way of the wicked leads them astray." Proverbs 12:26

REFLECTION:

1) Why is it important not to be a part of a cult?
2) How could the above scripture be interpreted when it comes to cults?
3) Have you ever known anyone in a cult? If so, did that person try to persuade you to join?
4) Are there any *good* cults for the Christian?

CHALLENGE:

* Read about cults to educate yourself.
* Make use of opportunities to hear talks by people who once had belonged to a cult and have now left.
* Talk to a Christian professional such as a policeman or minister about cults and how to avoid them.

The Horror of Terrorism

Take yourself back to September 11, 2001, when the horrible terrorist activity struck New York City's World Trade Center by hijacking airplanes and aiming those planes at innocent people. Chances are you remember only too well what you were doing at that time and how you felt. Perhaps you were grief stricken with disbelief. Or maybe you were angry. Or maybe you experienced sadness and anger mixed with feelings of panic and fear.

It's difficult to see terror bestowed on the United States, a country that has fought and maintained freedom for so long.

So why did God allow such a bad thing to happen in America? Were we not being good listeners? Surely, that's what Christians throughout the world wondered after hearing about the terrorists that September day.

Even so, as Christians we need to remind ourselves that the Bible doesn't say we won't face disaster from time to time while living on earth. In fact, it says just the opposite! Proverbs 21:8 says, "The way of the guilty is devious, but the conduct of the innocent is upright."

Our hope lies in the fact that Jesus Christ promised we can someday enter heaven's gates where no pain or sorrow or terrorist activity of any kind takes place. Heaven is beautifully described in the Bible, and it's obvious to see this is a place where happiness, peace, and joy surmount. Find comfort in that fact.

❖SCRIPTURE:

"I will praise the Lord, who counsels me; even at night my heart instructs me. I have set the Lord always before me. Because he is at my right hand, I will not be shaken.

"Therefore my heart is glad and my tongue rejoices; my body also will rest secure, because you will not abandon me to the grave, nor will you let your Holy One see decay. You have made known to me the path of eternal pleasures at your right hand." Psalm 16:7-11

CHALLENGE:

Be kind to someone by:
* Volunteering to donate blood for the sick
* Or offer some of your time to charity work

Author's note: I wrote the above devotion on September 12, 2001. It's hard to say what will happen in the days ahead but I'm deeply moved by the acts of Christianity already pouring through the United States and other countries across the world in the form of prayer groups, volunteer work, and numerous other charity acts to help the victim's families of this tragic event.

What About Suicide?

In the year 2000, suicide was the third leading cause of death in young people 15 to 24 years old, according to the National Institute of Mental Health statistics. One Internet article indicated that males carry out suicide at a rate four times to that of females, according to the American Association of Suicidology, a group dedicated to suicide prevention. This group also points out that no one knows how many survivors there are who lost a loved one to suicide, but a conservative estimate is 4.4 million Americans.

Josh, one of today's teens, tried to commit suicide twice. Once he slashed his wrists. His family found him and took him to the emergency room. Another time he overdosed on pills. Again, he survived. Listen to what he says now.

"I was one of the real lucky ones. I survived and enjoy life now," he said. "I want kids to know that no problem is too big for God."

Josh said he is confident he will never again consider suicide. He found the answer on how to face his problems—and enjoy life in Jesus Christ.

Now meet another teen, Erica. When she overdosed on pills, she died before her family found her. In cases like that, there's no turning back.

Naturally, Erica's parents were devastated. They were grief-stricken that they hadn't found her in time. For a long time they blamed themselves for her death. Of course, it wasn't their fault. With God's help, they are beginning to realize that fact.

Suicide is nothing new. Matthew 27:5 tells, "So Judas threw the money into the temple and left. Then he went away and hanged himself."

Numerous other examples of people committing suicide are in the Bible.

Listen to the good news. You don't have to commit suicide when you become overloaded with problems. You can find strength to go on no matter what problem you're facing because God will help if you call upon him. That's one of the wonderful promises from our Heavenly Father.

❖SCRIPTURE:

"The righteous cry out, and the Lord hears them; he delivers them from all their troubles. The Lord is close to the brokenhearted and saves those who are crushed in spirit. A righteous man may have many troubles, but the Lord delivers him from them all . . . " Psalms 34:17-19

REFLECTION:

1) Do you think every teen goes through difficult times when they feel helpless? Why or why not?
2) Have you ever thought of suicide? Why or why not?

CHALLENGE:

* If you face problems that overwhelm you right now, and you think suicide may be the answer, please *immediately* call someone for help. Can't think of anyone? Then call this hotline number: 1-800-784-2433. This is a hotline for people contemplating suicide. Notice this number is toll-free—just like God's grace!
* If you don't feel suicidal but you know someone who does, reach out to them. Today. Tomorrow may be too late. Tell them about the number above and speak to a professional.

BE MY ANCHOR, LORD

We have this hope as an anchor

for the soul, firm and secure.

Hebrews 6:19a

Worship Only God

I know a teenager who watched television every spare moment he had. He confessed to me that his "god" was television.

"I'm not saying watching television is wrong for everyone," Mark said. "It's not. I just know I became obsessed with television. I'd watch it before I left for school and after I got home until it was bedtime. I never accomplished anything and wasted lots of time in front of the TV."

Imagine Mark's disappointment when one day their television broke.

Months later, Mark had saved enough money to buy a new television set. But when he brought it home, a strange thing happened.

"I'd become used to living without television, and I realized it was such a good time, a quiet time, for me. I started a hobby and enjoyed the outdoors," he said.

Several months later, Mark heard about a needy family who moved into the neighborhood. Their belongings were destroyed in a house fire.

So what did Mark decide to do? He gave the family his television set! Mark's Christian parents were for the idea.

"This is for you," Mark said proudly to the family as he set the television set in middle of the living room. "I bought it with my money, and I want you to have it."

The family was stunned that a young man would be so thoughtful. They thanked him for the generous gift.

Now, isn't that a neat story? Mark turned his "god" into doing something good for someone in need.

❖SCRIPTURE:

"You shall have no other gods before me. You shall not make for yourself an idol in the form of anything in heaven above or on the earth beneath or in the waters below. You shall not bow down to them or worship them; . . . " Deut. 5:7-8

REFLECTION:

1) Do you have any "gods" or a "god" in your life?

2) If you do, what are they and how can you get rid of them?

CHALLENGE:

* Talk to a Christian youth group leader about having "gods" in your life.
* Discuss other "gods" with friends and what we can do to worship only one God, our Heavenly Father, who sent his son Jesus Christ to come to the earth and reveal the power of the Holy Spirit.

What's the Big Deal about Faith?

On a scale of one to ten, measure your faith. Now, how does your measurement look? Is it high or low?

If it's on the low side, good news. A deeper faith can fill your life. How? Take special note of the scripture in Romans 10:17 that says, "Consequently, faith comes from hearing the message, and the message is heard through the word of Christ." Romans 10:17.

That means every single day you can receive faith for whatever situation you may be facing by reading the Bible. Or maybe you're one of those people who think "real men" don't read the Bible. It's just the opposite! It takes a *man* to read and study God's word and to apply the teaching of Jesus Christ into his life.

But how can a person "get" faith after he fails an English test? you may wonder. Or is turned down for a date? Or can't get on the same wavelength with his parents?

Keep in mind that in Matthew 17:20 Jesus says, "Because you have so little faith. I tell you the truth, if you have faith as small as a mustard seed, you can say to this mountain, 'Move from here to there' and it will move. Nothing will be impossible for you."

Sometime look at a mustard seed. It's not big.

❖SCRIPTURE:

"Now faith is being sure of what we hope for and certain of what we do not see." Hebrews 11:1

REFLECTION:

1) Do you want faith in Jesus in your life? Why or why not?
2) Think of a Christian you know who has a deep faith. How would you classify that person? Fun to be with? Pleasant? Looks on the bright side? Encourages other people?

CHALLENGE:

Try one or more of our faith-builders that follow:

1) Today remind yourself that faith comes from God and can't be seen.
2) Tell a good friend about faith.
3) Read Hebrews (called the faith chapter in the Bible).

What's the Big Deal about Prayer?

Praying is something you may take for granted, but it's one of our greatest gifts from God. Think of how horrible things would be if we couldn't pray—that is if God didn't hear our thoughts, regardless if we prayed outloud or silently.

Life would be pretty scary that way. I heard Richard say he wouldn't want to go one day without prayer when he could ask God for help.

And, if you think about it, you probably feel the same way. So be grateful that you have access to God's hotline, toll-free number anytime. Don't be afraid to use it.

Maybe you're one of those people who's always in a hurry when you pray. You know, like when your teacher hands you a test paper and you forgot to study! Boy, you can sure pray then. But how about those times when everything is going okay? If you're like a lot of people, often you may not think to pray when things are on an even keel. Why bother God, you may figure, when you're happy?

As you grow in your Christian faith over the years, God wants to hear from you, whatever your frame of mind may be in. He cares.

It's not important about *how* you pray. It can be outloud. Or it can be silent. Whatever. So don't hesitate to develop a good prayer life. Real men pray.

❖SCRIPTURE:

"If my people, who are called by my name, will humble themselves and pray and seek my face and turn from their wicked ways, then will I hear from heaven and will forgive their sin and will heal their land." II Chronicles 7:14

REFLECTION:

1) On a scale of one to ten, how would you rate your prayer life?
2) If your prayer life is ranked low, ask yourself why. And what can you do about it?

3) If you gave yourself a good rating, that's great. Keep prayer in your life.

CHALLENGE:

* Take a moment right now, as you read this, to say a prayer. Then listen for God's answer. Listening is a big part of a good prayer life. I don't mean God will talk to you outloud (although he's been known to do that with some people), but if you're still and wait patiently, he will guide you.
* Think of your friends. Do any of them need a special prayer? If so, say a prayer for them.

Reflections

LQ

Lord, you have come to the seashore
asking me to follow you.
You have called out my name.
Docked in this harbor of life
are sailboats, rowboats and cruisers.
I have abandoned my small boat
as I seek to do your will.

ORDER FORM

Cut Me Some Slack, Lord
by Mary Ann Kerl
or for her companion book
Are You Listening, Lord?
Reflections for Christian Teen Girls

If unavailable at your favorite bookstore,
LangMarc Publishing will fill
your order within 24 hours.

— Postal Orders —
LangMarc Publishing
P.O. 90488
Austin, Texas 78709-0488
or call 1-800-864-1648
email: langmarc@booksails.com
Cut Me Some Slack, Lord: $9.95 + $2 postage
Are You Listening, Lord? $6.95 + $2 postage

Send _____ copies of *Cut Me Some Slack, Lord*
Send _____ copies of *Are You Listening, Lord?*

_____
_____
_____

Phone: _____

Check enclosed: _____

Credit Card: _____
_____ Expires: ____

Printed in the United States
18848LVS00001B/124-144